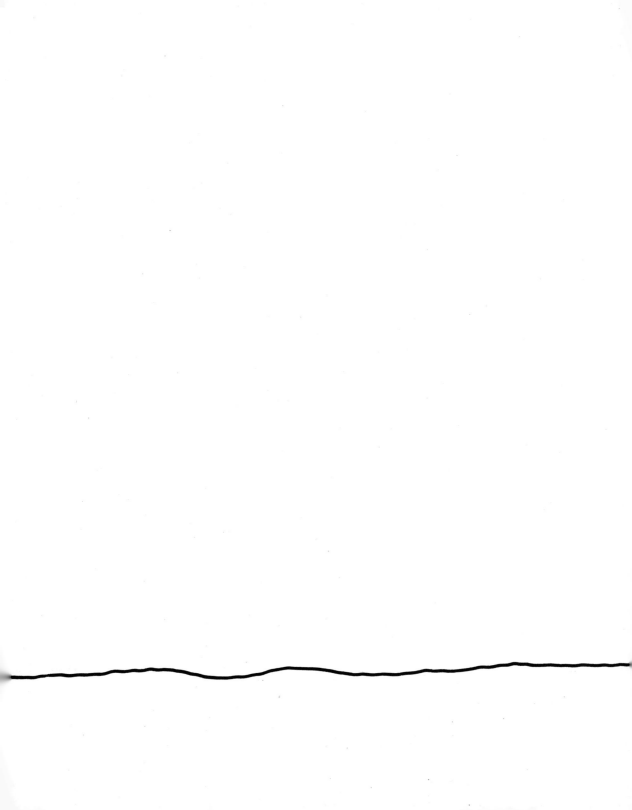

The Missing Piece

An Ursula Nordstrom Book

Shel Silverstein

THE MISSING PIECE

HarperCollins*Publishers*

THE MISSING PIECE

Library of Congress Catalog Card Number: 75-37408
ISBN 978-0-06-025671-5
ISBN 978-0-06-025672-2 (lib. bdg.)

12 13   LP/WOR   40 39 38 37

for Gerry

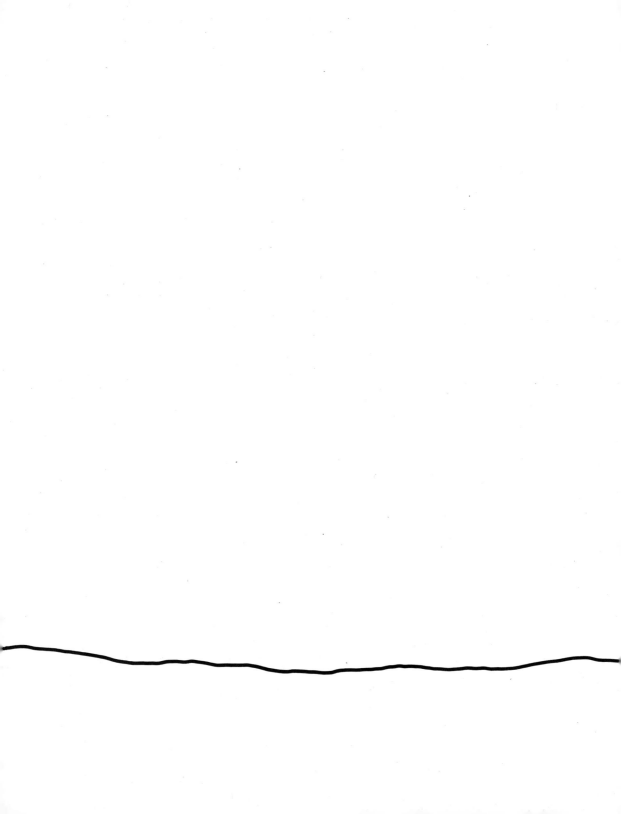

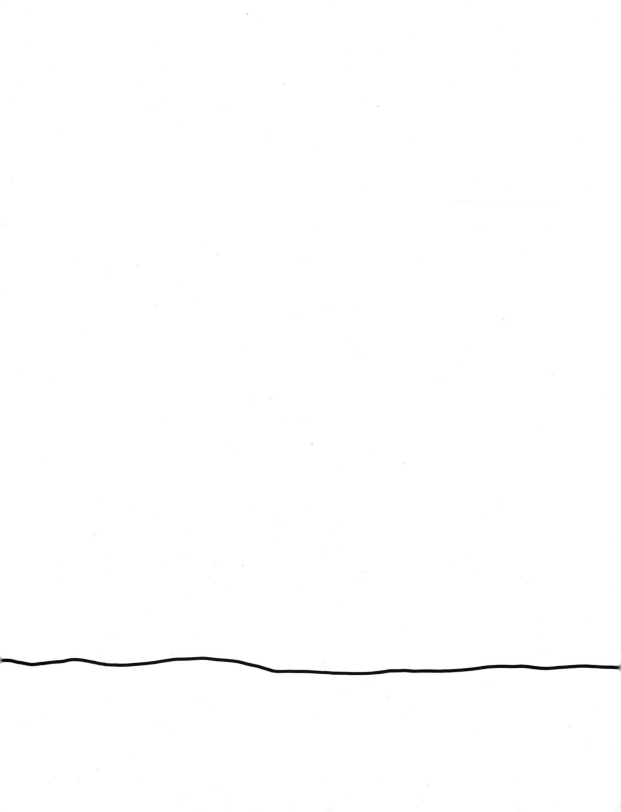

It was missing a piece.
And it was not happy.

So it set off in search
of its missing piece.

And as it rolled
it sang this song—

"Oh I'm lookin' for my missin' piece
I'm lookin' for my missin' piece
Hi-dee-ho, here I go,
Lookin' for my missin' piece."

Sometimes it baked in the sun

but then the cool rain would come down.

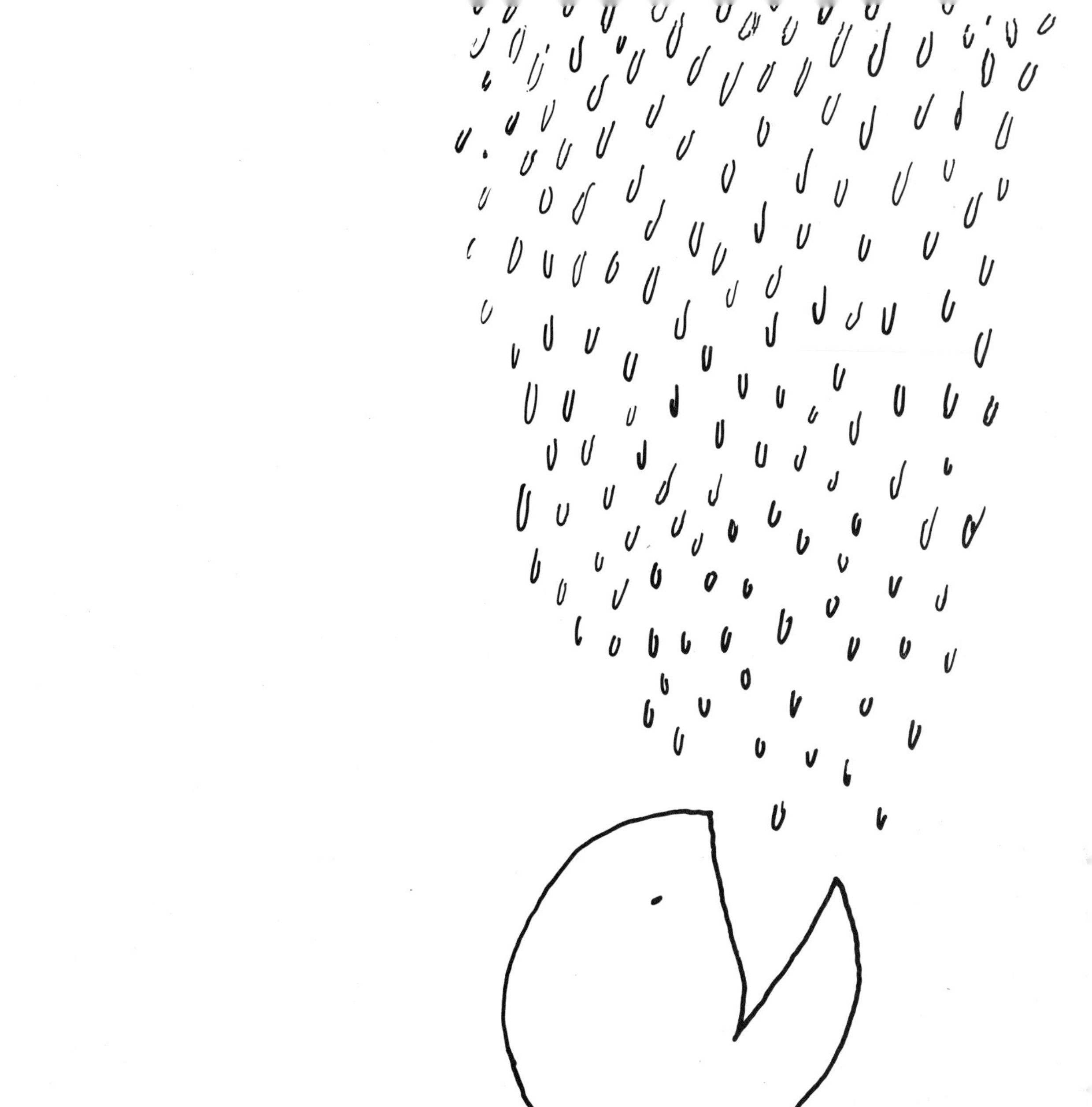

And sometimes it was frozen by the snow
but then the sun would come and warm it again.

And because it was missing a piece
it could not roll very fast
so it would stop
to talk to a worm

or smell a flower

and sometimes it would pass a beetle

and sometimes the beetle
would pass it

and this was the best time of all.

And on it went,
over oceans

"Oh I'm lookin' for my missin' piece
Over land and over seas
So grease my knees and fleece my bees
I'm lookin' for my missin' piece."

through swamps and jungles

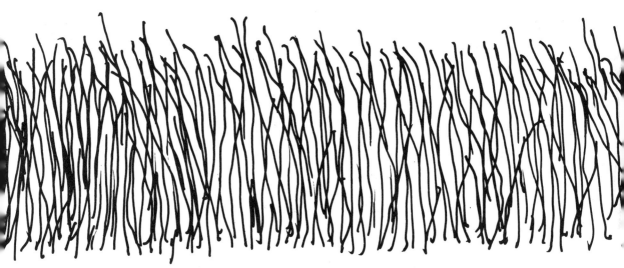

up mountains

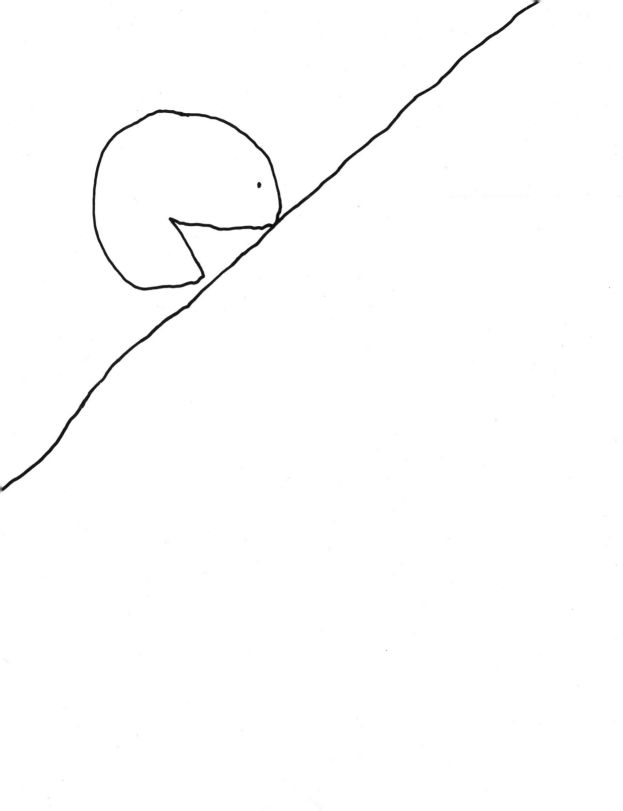

and down mountains

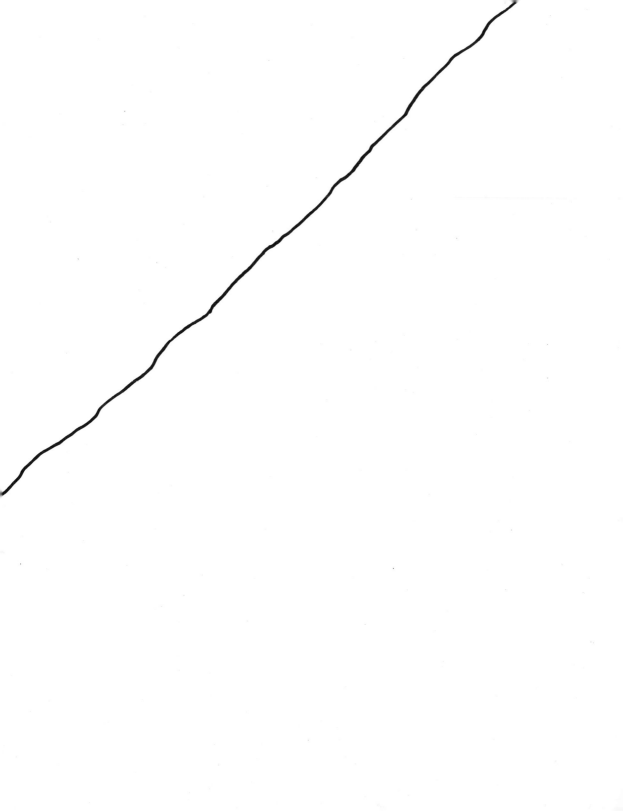

Until one day, lo and behold!

"I've found my missin' piece," it sang,
"I've found my missin' piece
So grease my knees and fleece my bees
I've found my..."

"Wait a minute," said the piece.
"Before you go greasing your knees
and fleecing your bees...

"I am not your missing piece.
I am nobody's piece.
I am my own piece.
And even if I was
somebody's missing piece
I don't think I'd be yours!"

"Oh," it said sadly,
"I'm sorry to have bothered you."
And on it rolled.

It found another piece

but this one was too small.

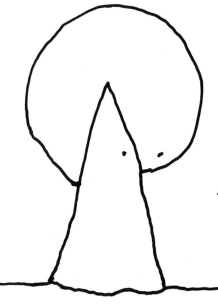

And this one was too big

this one was a little too sharp

and this one was too square.

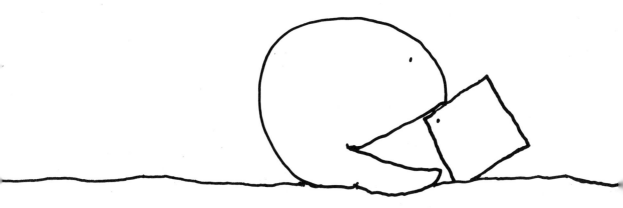

One time it seemed
to have found
the perfect piece

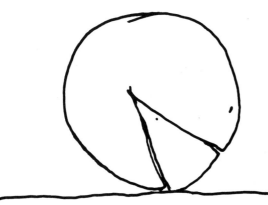

but it didn't hold it tightly enough

and lost it.

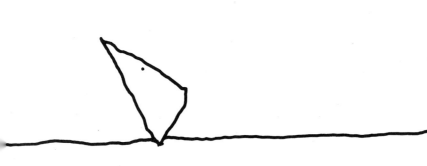

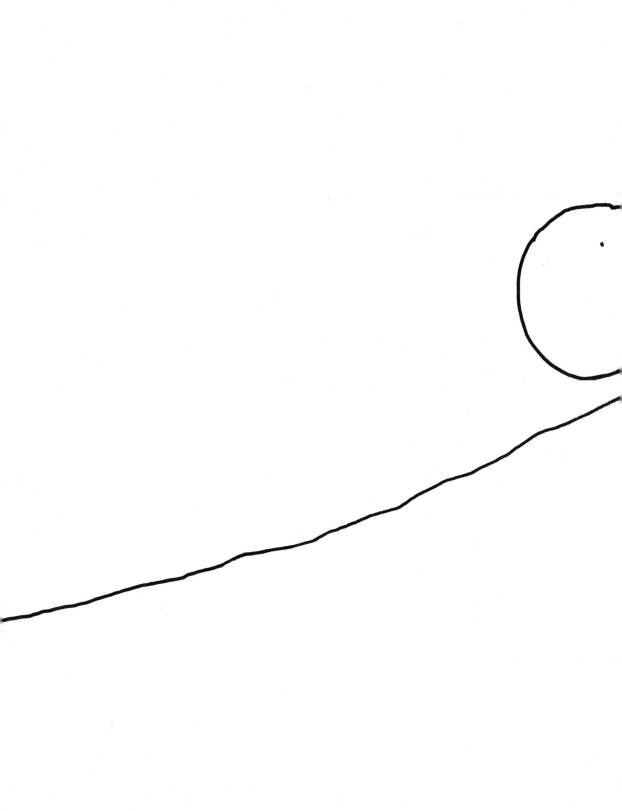

Another time
it held too tightly

and it broke.

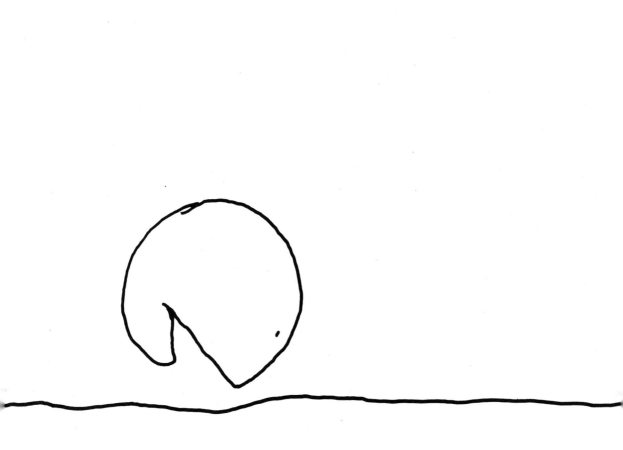

So on and on it rolled,

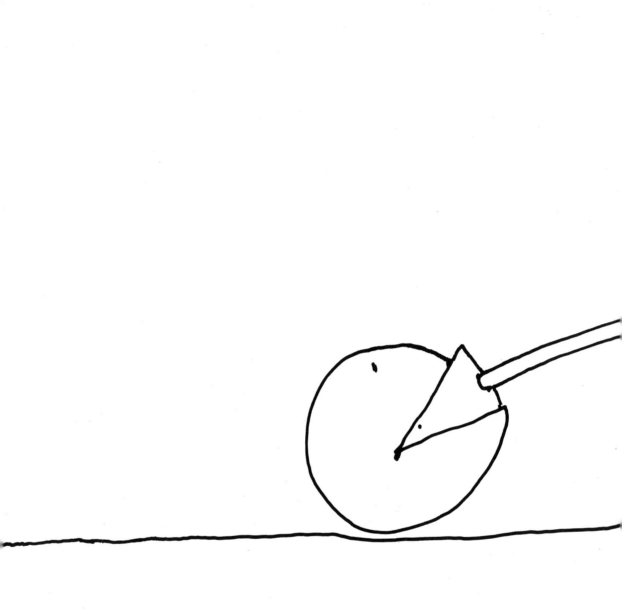

having adventures

falling into holes

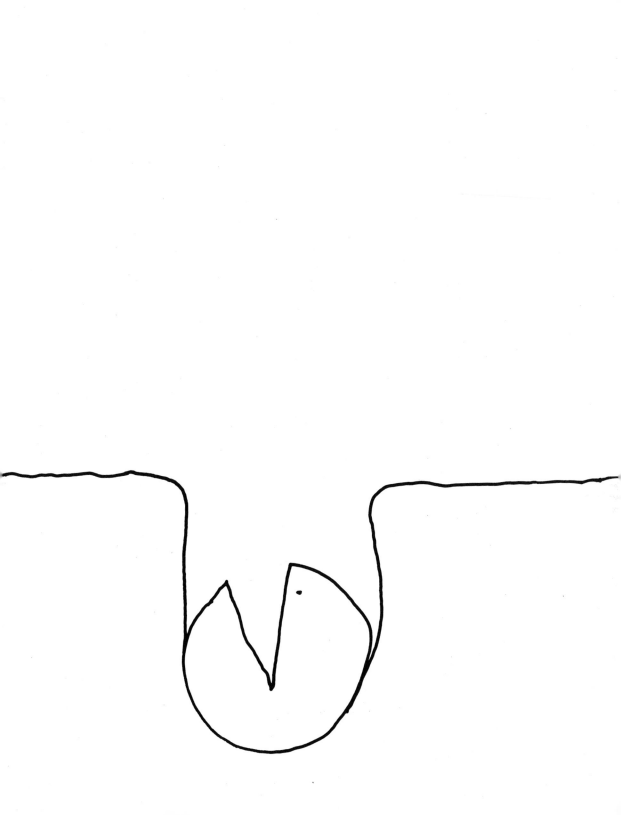

and bumping into stone walls.

And then one day it came upon
another piece that seemed
to be just right.

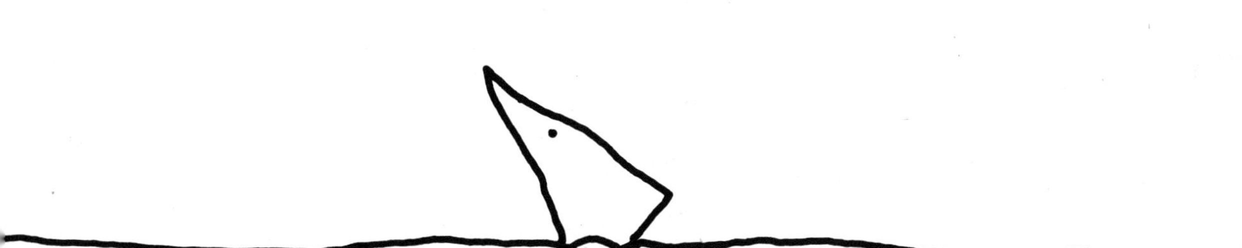

"Hi," it said.

"Hi," said the piece.

"Are you anybody else's missing piece?"

"Not that I know of."

"Well, maybe you want to be your own piece?"

"I can be someone's and still be my own."

"Well, maybe you don't want to be mine."

"Maybe I do."

"Maybe we won't fit...."

"Well..."

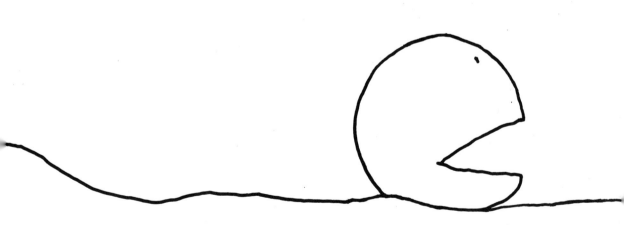

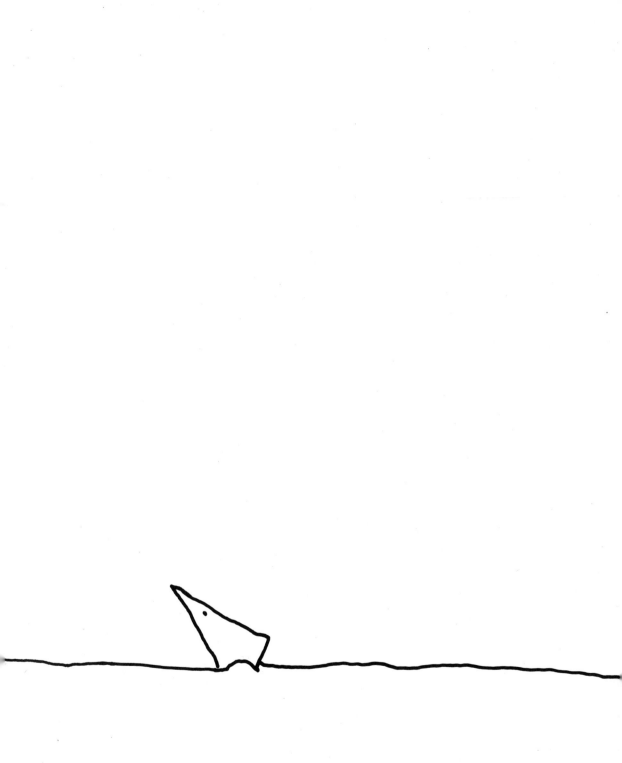

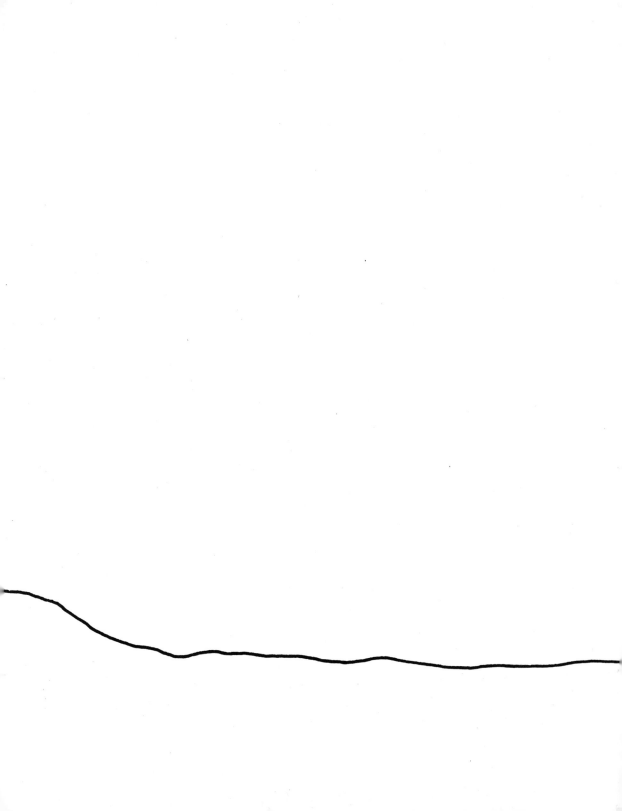

"Hummm?"
"Ummmm!"

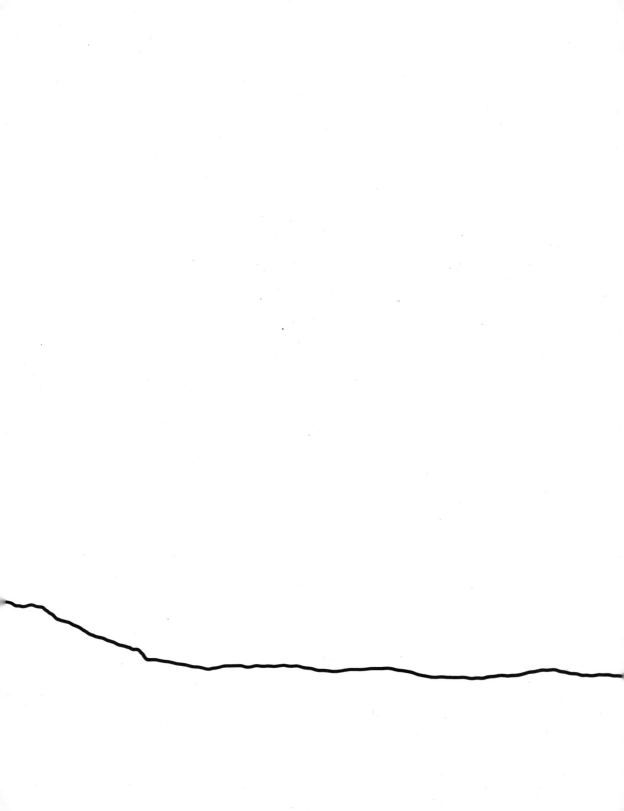

It fit!
It fit perfectly!
At last! At last!

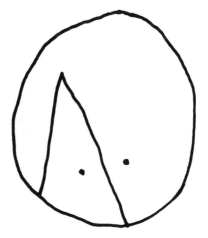

And away it rolled
and because it was
now complete,
it rolled faster
and faster.
Faster than it had
ever rolled before!

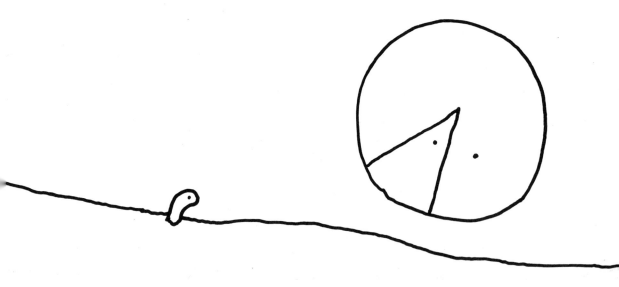

So fast that it could not stop
to talk to a worm

or smell a flower

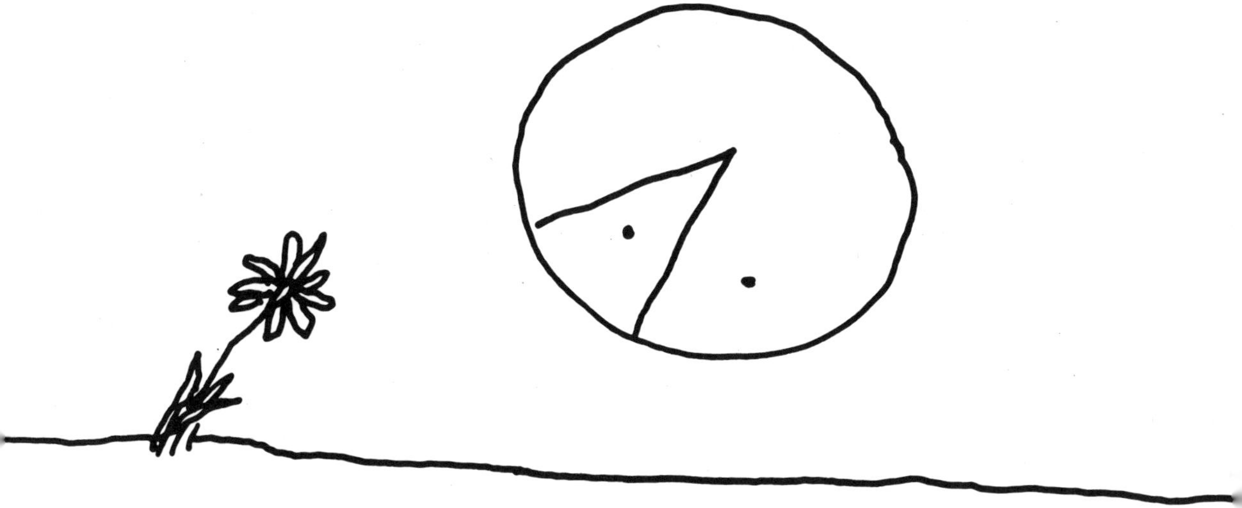

too fast for a butterfly to land.

But it *could* sing its happy song,
at last it could sing
"I've found my missing piece."

And it began to sing—
  "I've frown my nizzin' geez
  Uf vroun my mitzin' brees
  So krease ny meas
  An bleez ny drees
  Uf frown..."

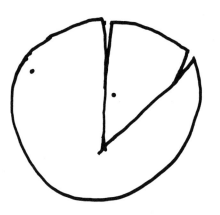

Oh my, now that
it was complete
it could not sing at all.

"Aha," it thought.
"So *that's* how it is!"

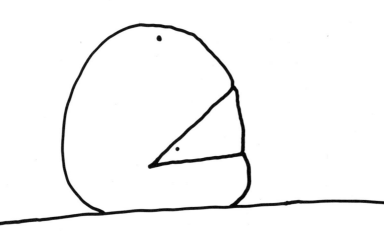

So it stopped rolling...

and it set the piece down gently,

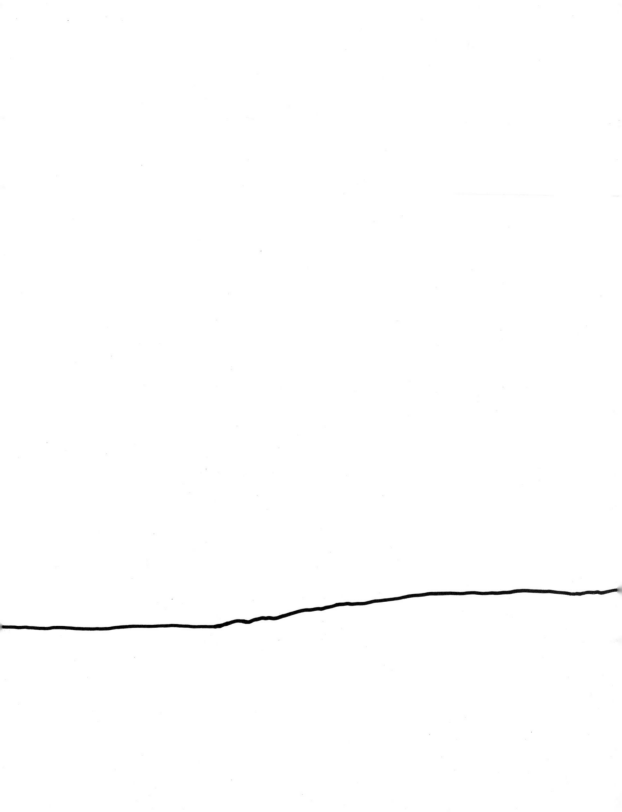

and slowly rolled away

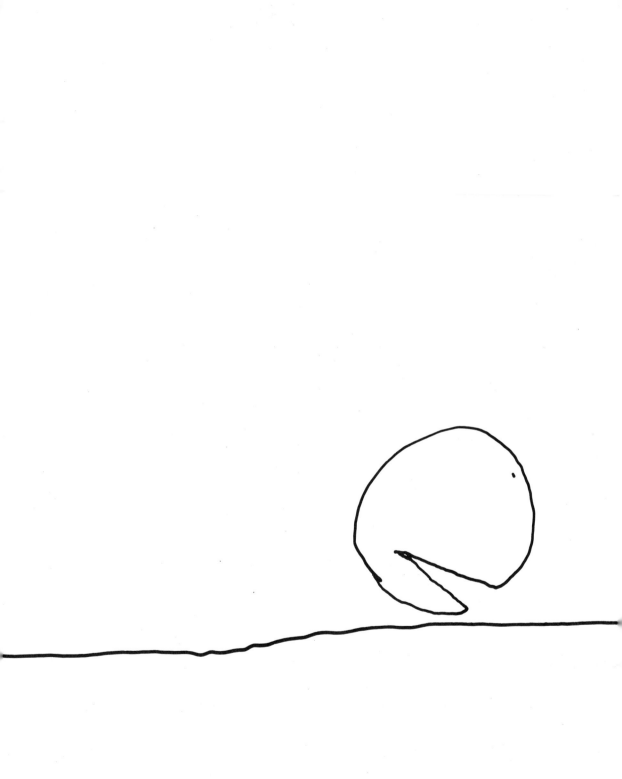

and as it rolled it softly sang—

"Oh I'm lookin' for my missin' piece
I'm lookin' for my missin' piece
Hi-dee-ho, here I go,
Lookin' for my missin' piece."

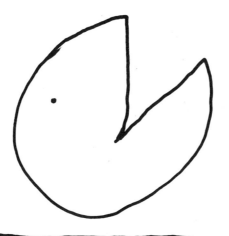

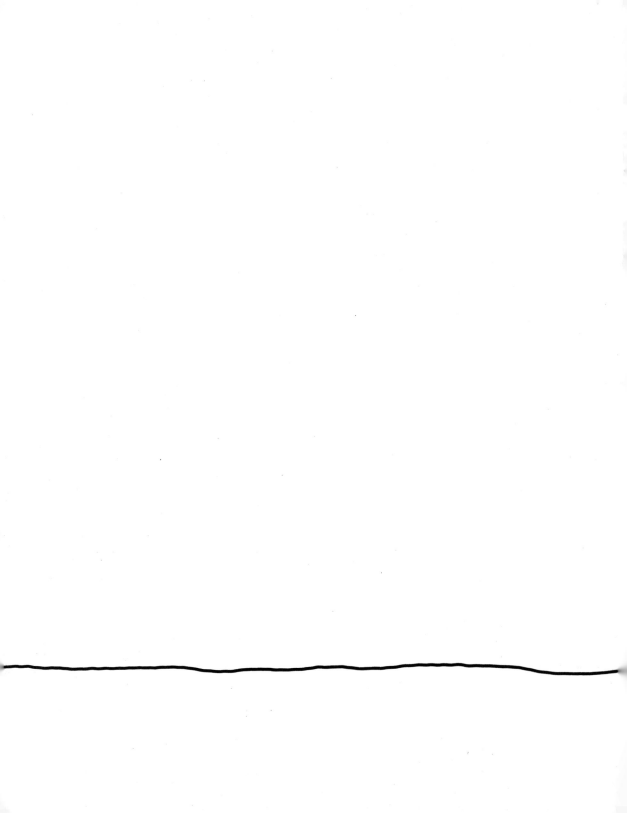